THUNDER THREE

AND THE SECRET CASTLE

PRANJAL SHUKLA

Contents

Preface

Firstly, I want to thank god who is giving me the strength to write this book.

Secondly, thanks to Ritu Sharma Ma'am, who is my English tutor. Because of her, I wrote this book.

After that, thank Mradu Shukla for helping me with this book. She's my younger sister who made all the illustrations for this book.

And thanks to Dad (Anuj Shukla) and Mom (Anshu Shukla), who gave me the motivation to write this book.

And last but not least my friends support me a lot.

Thanks a lot for helping me to write this book

Prologue

Rubal - The Main Hero

Blaze - Rubal's Best friend

Sherlin - Rubal's friend

Simon The Monk - The Head Master of Romana Gaur School and the Monk of Rubal, Sherlin and Blaze

Puneet - Father of Rubal

Neetu - Mother of Rubal

Sathya - Father of Blaze

Gayathri - Mother of Blaze

Denial - A student who studies in Romana Gaur School and his biggest enemy was Rubal, Blaze and Sherlin

Professor Abhishek - Professor of Romana Gaur School, who teaches about Weapon

Professor Mradu - Professor of Romana Gaur School, who teaches about Black Magic

Professor Bhist - Professor of Romana Gaur School, who teaches about Defence

WhiteWash Venom Spite - The main Villain

Amon - Right Hand of WhiteWash Venom Spite

Ramon - Left Hand of WhiteWash Venom Spite

How I Got An Idea To Make This Book

I am telling you how I got the idea to write this book.
My friend Abheek, Swastik and I had an English tuition class in which we used to write a story on our own and we have to tell our teacher Ritu Sharma Ma'am. Due to this activity, I could write this story. One day in the tuition class, Abheek started to tell the story of three friends who were having superpowers and every week he told the next part of this story and the title was " The Worthy 3 ". I was impressed by the title of the story as it sounds splendid!.
One day, Swastik, Abheek and I came to our society playground and I said to them " I have a great idea! wanna want to listen to that? "
"Yes-yes why not," Abheek said to me. I suggested to them " We all three friends can write a book related to three superheroes and we can write our own book on this topic". Because we were three friends and wanted to write three books on three superheroes.
So, we started to write the book. When we were writing our books, every day we came to the playground and asked each other how many pages we had written in our book and everyone shared his story with us. That time, we were very excited.
Before the summer break, everyone wrote 1 to 2 chapters for their book. Summer breaks were near and our strategy was to complete our books during the summer breaks. Yes, we achieved this goal also. While we were doing such activities, we didn't tell Ritu ma'am as we kept it as a surprise for her.

We all enjoyed writing our books and we had a

great experience.

I want to give a special thanks to Mradu Shukla, she is my younger sister who made all the illustrations for this book as she did for my first book " Jack The Killer "

I

The Beginning of the Journey

That was a murky day, everyone's eyes were stuck on a circular which was shown by their class teacher. Everyone was watching it too carefully that anyone can hear winds voice

" School has organised a trip to Romana and those whosoever are interested in that can submit 800ruppes for this trip," said The Class Teacher

Ma'am, said Rubal, May I ask you something?

Rubal was a boy with long pure black hair, brownish eyes and with a ring in which there is a purple colour stone which was there in his right hand from birth.

Yes, tell me

When we are going to Romana?

Ms Curie grinned and said " Rubal, we will go there on the 29th of December means after 4 days"

And suddenly the bell rings!, and everyone scurries up and packs their bags and all start running outside of the classroom, soon Rubal came out of the class after completing his quarries from Ms Curie.

When Rubal came out of the school, he found his old friend " Blaze "

Hey Blaze! How are you?

Oh. Rubal, Hello! my friend

Both were very excited and then Rubal asked him a question " Did your class teacher told you about the trip? "

Um... Romana one?

Yes!, said Rubal, so will you go on that trip?

Ah... I don't know, I have to take permission from my dad said Blaze, well are you going on the trip?

Yes! of course, My dad will undoubtedly permit me for that

Wow!, how lucky you are. said Blaze

After that, they both went there home

The Next day...

Outside the school, they met again but this time a different smile was on Blaze's face which Rubal had never seen before.

You are looking so content, what happens? Rubal asked

Rubal-Rubal, M-My dad has permitted me for going to Romana! Blaze said in a thrilling way

Wow, nice. Now we both will enjoy it there! said Rubal

The Blaze asked Rubal " Do you know some philosophers believe that Romana is a perplexing place and their people get superpowers"

Hah, Rubal murmured, " I don't believe in these things, there is nothing as superpowers exist in this world and Blaze you are not a kid who believes in these frictional things"

Um. It's your thinking, but I believe this thing said Blaze politely

Oh, so will see there that could we find any perplexing thing? said Rubal

After 3 days...

The sun was shining, the clouds were looking golden and the wind was flowing, then suddenly Rubal's alarm started screaming and Rubal woke up and sat on the bed and his eyes firstly goes on the calendar and the date was 2 Jan and then his eyes move towards the left side of the room and he watched the clock which was hanging on the wall, the time was 6 o'clock and then a giant smile came on Rubal's face.

Near 7 o'clock, Rubal was ready to go to his school and then he touched his mom and dad's feet Dan blessed him and he said " Today is a very momentous day in your life my boy, go and rock in Romana! " at the time Rubal was about to say something but school bus arrived and he left the home.

At 8 o'clock, They reached school and from there they sat on another bus and after almost 3 hours they all reached Romana. There the temperature was above 30 and a warm wind was flowing everywhere was sand and sand, in front, there was a Calavera future zoo and then suddenly the land started moving and suddenly Rubal fall down, he screamed " aaaaaaaaaaaaaaa! " and suddenly he saw that he was standing somewhere and he said " We-Where I am? "

And suddenly a voice came from somewhere " You are in Romana training centre" and then Rubal said " Who-Who are you and where are-are you...?! " and while speaking Rubal found that a bit far away someone else was there and a sensation came in Rubal's soul that was saying that "this is Blaze" and as he moves forward and he found Blaze there! who was crying " Mom... Dad" and Rubal started laughing " hahaha, Blaze you are in 5th standard but you are still a lament as a kid!" then Blaze moves his head towards Rubal and there were a lot of tears on Blaze's face and his nose was running but when he saw Rubal, his crying face changes into a smiling face and his running nose again went in the nostrils " Rubal- Rubal you are here! "

Yes, my friend

And then suddenly a screaming voice came from somewhere and a girl falls down near Rubal and Blaze, both laughed a lot.

Hey! Stop it said the girl

Haha... Well, who are you? asked Rubal

Hey, she is Sherlin said, Blaze

What! how do you know her?

Bro, she studies in my class only, and then Sherlin said " Leave all the things, first of all where we are!? "

And suddenly the place started to quiver " Wha-What is happening? said Rubal. And suddenly a man came in front of them and he was flying, he was wearing an orange colour cloth as Monk used to wear it.

Who-Who are you? All the 3 asked

I am Monk of your parents and I had given them some superpowers from which they have protected the world but now we need your type of superhero who will save this world from wickedness.

Nah! my buddy, Monk if it is like that then show some superpowers to us said Rubal

See Rubal, What I told you, now you have to agree

Are you mad!?, said, Sherlin, You can't able to see that he is flying!...

Monk interrupted and said, " It's fine, you all are just kids, let me show you some powers" then Monk appear a big giant rock, which came there and was flying in the sky and an orange-type weapon came into Monk's forefinger which was spinning and was looking like Krishna's chakra and then Monk flung the chakra towards the rock and then some blades came out of orange and the scene was like a Bollywood film and in a second that orange made the huge rock into small fragments and Rubal doesn't waste a second and said, " Sorry Monk, I misjudge your powers, now I understood."

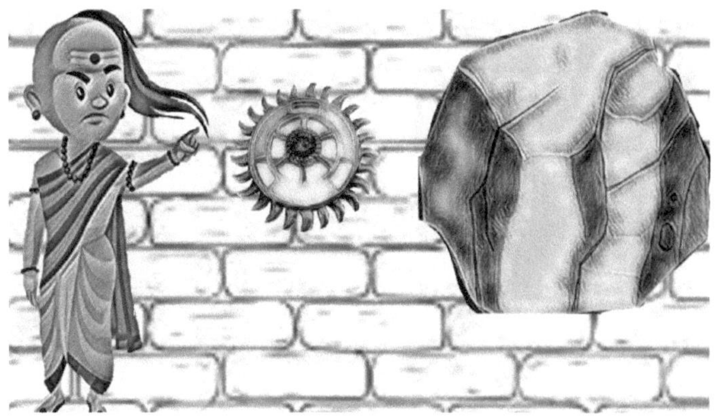

And then Monk said " Now, I want to tell you that this is not compulsory that you can get these powers, for that you need to be worthy of it"

But how we will be worthy of it!? asked Blaze

You have to do a lot of practice for that and then I will give you a test and if you passed in that then you will get the superpowers. said Monk

Oh, I am ready for that, but what's your name Monk? asked Sherlin

Well, my name was Simon

"Was"!? said Rubal, it is, not was

Monk laughed and said " It was, now I am dead "

And when all the three listens to this they stared at the monk in a perplexed way. Wha-What! said all three, how is it possible that you are still here if you are dead!

II

The Story of "Simon, the Monk"

Okay, so let me tell you my story. A long time ago, um... around 103 years back, godsend me on the earth like godsends everyone but the only difference was that I know the task which God told me to do, and second thing was that I was having superpowers...

Everyone was listening carefully and suddenly Blaze sneezes " aaaaa. chu!"

Off o Blaze! What you are doing said Rubal

Um, sorry I was not able to regulate it.

Hey, both of you please maintain hush! and let Monk continue his story said, Sherlin

Just wait!, Sherlin, said Rubal. Monk, till now I don't watch any evil, who was trying to demolish the earth.

Monk smiled and said " Nice question, these evil attacks on earth in every 50 years and try to capture earth and soon 50 years will be over and then they will thrash on earth again.

But if it is like that then why they don't attack now!?, why do they wait for 50 years. said Sherlin

Last time we defeated them but can't able to kill the main immorality and they use to take 50 years for preparation and that's why soon they will again try to capture earth, said Monk.

So, where I was... oh yea! I was having superpowers and I was born in Romana means here only and at the time I was having all the powers, which I soon divided into my pupils, so after that when I was 15 or 16 first-time evils attacked the earth and at the time I defeated them as a piece of cake and as I told you early that they attack after 50 years, so after 45 years, I was almost 60 and I was old enough but I was robust as when I was 15, but I was knowing that now evils will be much powerful and that's why I trained your grandfathers and mothers and after 5 years we fought the war, we won but Rubal's grandmother and Sherlin's grandfather got martyred

But-But my dad and mom use to tell me that My grandmother was died because of cancer. said Rubal

And same with me said, Sherlin.

Yes, because if they told you this thing and in case you told someone that your mom, dad and grandfather or mother are superheroes then it may create a big problem. said, Monk

And were my grandfather and mother alive? asked Blaze

Rubal said " When did you meet your grandparent last time? "

Um... A month ago

So, how will they die in that war!?

Ops, sorry I don't think about that said Blaze

So, no more discussions, said Monk, after that there's a rule that the maximum age of retirement is 60 and the minimum age is 30 and when you take retirement then your power will be taken back. And soon your grandparents take retirement and after that, it was the turn of your mom and dad and when I teleported them into this lab and I was telling them about superpowers, suddenly a right hand of Whitewash who's the boss of all the evils, and that Right Hand of Whitewash shoot cannonball on me and I hit on the wall of this lab and the bricks plummet on me and the weight of the walls were thousand tons and then I die...

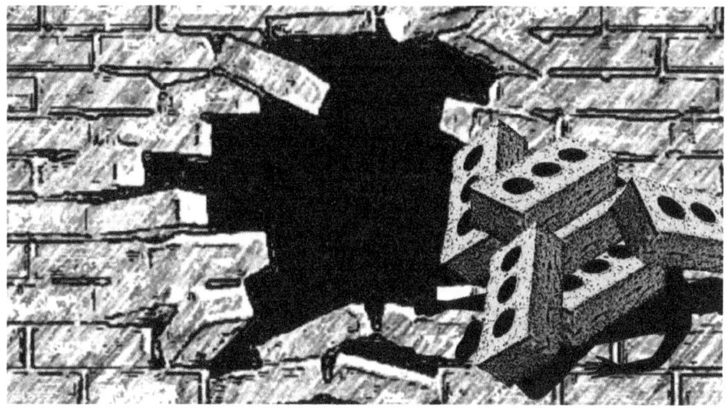

Everyone was silent and frozen the silence was too much that they all could hear lava's voice which was just below the Lab, then Sherlin broke up the silence and said " but how you are still here after the death and what happened to our mom and dad after you were dead!?

After a few seconds, Monk spoke " As, when I was born on the earth, I take an oath that I will do my work till then the earth will be 100% secured and that's why my soul doesn't get the peace that's why my soul is still on the earth and if you talk about your mom and dad, the right hand of Whitewash didn't spoil your mom and dad as he thinks that now " what can these children do? " so that's how I trained them and we also fought a war against them and we won but can't able to kill Whitewash. And that's how the story ends. Now you all have to choose a weapon by yourself and you have to practise for a year and then there will be a test.

What! for a year, so when we will going to study and our mom and dad will be also worried for us, cried Rubal.

Don't worry for study, and your mom and dad were already knowing this thing, so don't need to worry about that. said Monk, after that he clapped 3 times and a lot of weapons came there

III

The Training (first year)

After that, there were a lot of weapons came and Monk said " you all have to choose one-one weapon for yourself" and in few minutes all the 3 chooses their weapons and after that Monk said " Now, show your weapons to me" and then Rubal took out an orange and said this is my weapon, Monk.

Suddenly Sherlin and Blaze started to chuckle and said " You find an orange only, are you going to eat it!"

No, said Rubal, It is not a habitual orange and you can see it is 3 times bigger than a normal orange and now let me show its power, then Rubal flung the weapon and in a second, the orange razes thousands of tons of wall in 2 pieces and then it again come back and started spinning at Rubal's forefinger at the time Sherlin and Blaze's mouth was opened and their eyes were stuck on that Orange and their hands were shrinking.

We-We are sorrowful Rubal, said, Blaze

At that time, a small grin came on Rubal's face and he said, "Oh, that's ok, in friendship no thanks and no sorry."

After that Sherlin said " now let me show you my power after that Sherlin took out a pair of gulps and she said to Monk " May you place some objects here" then Monk placed 50 television and some trucks and then Sherlin wear the gulps and then she moved her hand upwards and soon all the television and trucks started flying but suddenly they all plummet again on the ground.

Ahh! it's arduous to handle them said, Sherlin

Yea, that's why you all have to do a lot of practice said, Monk

After that everyone was silent for a few seconds, but Blaze broke up the silence and said " May I show my weapon now? "

Yea said Rubal, why not?

And then Blaze took out a wiper and said " This is my weapon"

Suddenly Sherlin laughed and said " What! Wiper. a weapon! are you doing to clean the floor " and in a second she started shouting " Leave this wiper! or else because of you our image will become worst!"

No, said Blaze

Suddenly Sherlin interrupted and said " Yea, I know this you are just a witless boy, learn something from Rubal"

Sherlin! stop busting my chops! it's just like your orange, after that Blaze, after that he pressed a button which was on the wiper and suddenly the wiper started opening from the middle and a cannon came out of it and then Blaze shoot the cannon at the wall and a hollow formed on it.

Did you see that? said Blaze

Yes-Yes! said Sherlin, yea you are correct it is also a robust weapon...

When Blaze heard this thing, he chuckles

Then Monk interrupted and said " Now you have to do training and once it will complete then I will give you a task and you have to complete it! but remember the practice can take more than a year.

What! Blaze interrupted, more than a year! then what will happen to our study?

Don't worry about that, I have already told you!, said Monk, now your main focus should be " to be the master of your weapon" and now I will tell the thing on which you need to do work " Rubal you have to work on the control of your weapon and also on the accuracy, while Blaze you also have to work on accuracy and Sherlin you have to work on holding the objects in the weapon and throw it on the enemies"

Ok Monk said all the 3 at once

After that...

Monk started murmuring something and a greyish power started rotating around Rubal, Blaze and Sherlin and suddenly all the 3 teleported to a Training area when all the 3 entered the training centre, there were a lot of rooms! in which there are different-different practises to do, all were very obligated and soon all the 3 goes into different rooms. Rubal went into a room where some dummies were having some machine and from that arrows can be shot out, then Rubal opened his forefinger and trikol appeared at his figure and he throws it towards the dummies and suddenly the dummies started firing arrows towards Rubal and one by one Rubal cut all the arrows and then by mistake the orange hit a dummy and the dummy cut into 2 pieces

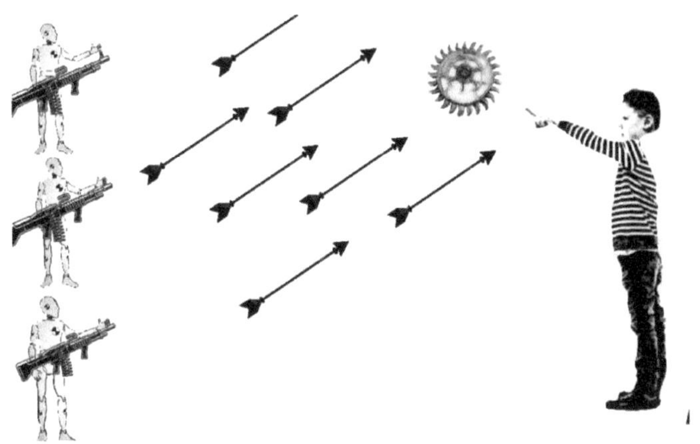

"opposes" Rubal murmured

And suddenly the dummy which has been cut stops shooting but the left dummies shoot arrows at a faster rate. At the time Rubal understand that he has to cut dummies and as he will cut them the left dummies will shoot at a faster rate after some time the fire rate of the arrows was too fast and an arrow came near Rubal and he shouted " ahhhhhh...!" but as the arrow struck Rubal, nothing happened to Rubal! and after that, he took out the arrow which was stucking in Rubal right hand and he flung it, soon Rubal realized that it was a fake arrow for practice.

Meanwhile, Blaze was also practising to have better aim, some dummies were shooting fake cannonballs and Blaze was tackling them and razing the dummy.

While Sherlin was practising picking up the objects.

IV

The Training Ends

So, the days went on...

After a year...

The 3 were prepared and became masters in using their weapons.

"Monk, we have been prepared and now you can take our test," said Rubal

Oh, nice! so now it's your test. In this test, there is a castle and there are 5000 people, who are trying to capture the castle, your task is to save the castle from the people...

5000! Rubal interrupted, how can we fight against 5000 people?!

With the help of your weapons and remember the people are having swords, bows and arrows, and last but not least they have cannons.

At that time all the 3 superheroes' eyes teared up as they know that they can't defeat 5000 people! After that Blaze and Sherlin said " We can't fight in this war and if we fight, then we shall die"

I never visualize this thing from you both!, said Rubal, It's just a small war and if you are fearful of that, then how are we going to fight again the main evil, don't forget our ancestors have also given their life for saving our present, and now we have to fight to save our future generation. Pick up your weapons and combat again those 5000 people!

Sorry, Rubal, said Blaze, I can't fight

Oh, then give me your weapon and go away! I will fight against them

And suddenly, Sherlin said, " I will fight!"

Then both Rubal and Sherlin stared at Blaze

Why are you watching me? said Blaze, but no reply came and they continuously stared at Blaze then Blaze look here and there and said " Ok, then I will fight"

That's nice said Rubal

After that Monk, place a castle there. The Castle was made of bricks and there was a big entrance gate, and there were some stairs from which anyone can reach on the 1st floor.

After that, they all came to Castel and at that time only, thousands of people started moving toward the castle.

Then Rubal ran onto the first floor! and he throw his "trikol" toward the people, he moves it right and left and from that almost 700 people were killed. Then Blaze took out his wiper and shoot the cannonball at the tremendous army and from that 150 people died after that Sherlin came out of the castle and she uses her power from which nearby big rock started flying in the sky and she throw them at the gigantic army and many people die in that, but soon the huge army came near the castle and they started breaking the door! and then Blaze started throwing cannonballs at the people which were near the gate but from that, a lot of cracks started coming on the gate and if Blaze doesn't stop then the gate will soon break and Rubal understood that thing, he said " Blaze! just stop or you may break the door.

So, what should I do!? aksed, Blaze

And suddenly an arrow hit Sherlin, " Ahh. Ahh" she screamed

Oh no!, an arrow hit's Sherlin leg, I have to go, and till then Blaze you make a big hole around the castle so that more soldiers can't come near the castle, Said Rubal

And then He ran towards Sherlin and Blaze started making big holes near the castle. But meanwhile, the soldiers broke up the gate and entered the castle!

Oh no!, Rubal you go and fight them, don't worry about me said, Sherlin

And then Rubal took out his trikol and throw it at the soldiers and one by one he killed more than 30 soldiers! but at the end, a soldier shoots a poison arrow toward Rubal and which hits Rubal's hand

Oh no, ahh... it's to pa-panic and after that, a fright started coming into Rubal's heart

And then Blaze saw Rubal and Sherlin were injured and shoot a cannonball towards the man who shoot a poison arrow at Rubal and all the soldiers were dead, those were in the castle and then Blaze came " Oh no, you both got injured!"

Blaze-Blaze did you make the hole? asked Rubal

Yes-Yes, my friend, now don't need to take anxiety.

And after that Blaze remove arrows from Rubal's hand and Sherlin's leg and flung them on the ground

But suddenly a blaring voice came from somewhere and Rubal felt like a bomb has been exposed near them and Rubal was right

After this, Blaze went to the 1st floor, he saw that the huge army started firing cannons.

Oh, no! they have started firing cannons and if we don't stop them, then the castle will be destroyed!.

I'm coming to kill them, Blaze, said Rubal, till then you to fire cannon on them.

And one by one the big army was shooting cannons and from that big cracks started coming on the castle wall. And then Rubal came to the 1st floor and throw his "trikol" from which one by one he was cutting cannonballs

When both Blaze and Rubal were fighting against the big army valiantly suddenly a cannon ball came near them and they both didn't notice it suddenly Rubal's eyes went on the cannonball which was coming towards them but that was too late, now Rubal and Blaze can't defend themself from the cannonball and Rubal felt that now he will be dead and he closed his eyes but what's that! after few seconds Rubal opened his eyes and he saw that the cannonball was flying in the sky, and one by one all the cannonballs which were lying near castle started flying

Blaze said to Rubal " See at the door!"

When Rubal saw at the gate, there was standing Sherlin, who was flying around 50 to 60 cannonballs and then she throws them at the huge army which was only left with less than a thousand people and soon the whole army was destroyed with the help of cannonballs.

Bravo!, we did it, Blaze said to Rubal

Oh, finally we won the war said, Blaze, but Sherlin you did a fantastic job

Yea, if she was not there then we may die said Rubal

Thanks, but you both also did splendid work said, Sherlin

Then Simon appears there and said " Well done, you have passed your test" now you will get these powers permanently till then you are not retired, and now it's your time to return home but don't forget to practise and also remember that never tell anyone that you have superpowers. And as you have passed your test, now I will increase your weapon power as much as I can.

After that, Monk increased the power of their weapon and Now Rubal's trikol can make a big bubble which will work as a defence object and now Rubal trikol can throw poison, fire and electric arrows. While Blaze wiper can now throw one more type of cannonball which is 10 times more powerful than the earlier weapon and Sherlin's gulps now have a range that she can set the distance that how far she wants to throw that object and the range will be 10 meters to 2 kilometres. Now this was the first year of your training and in this year you 3 became master of your weapon, but now there will be a 2months break and after that, you have to come again to Romana and this time there will be more people who will study with you and everyone will have different-different groups.

At that time everyone was happy but also sad as they have lived with Monk for a year.

V

Back to Home

After that, all the 3 were teleported to their homes, while when Rubal got teleported, he couldn't see anyone at home. He moves a bit and he saw that his mom and dad were watching television.

Mom and Dad, Rubal said

Suddenly Puneet (Rubal's dad) and Neetu (Rubal's mom) moves their head backwards and when Neetu saw Rubal, her eyes fill with tears and when Rubal saw tears in his mother's eyes he ran toward his mother and hugged her tightly after that Puneet asked: " Did you passed in the test?"

Ye-yes! dad said Rubal

Well done my boy! and aren't you going to show me your weapon? asked Puneet

Yea dad said Rubal, just wait. Meanwhile, Neetu goes from there into the kitchen to make something for Rubal.

After Rubal closed his thumb and all figures except his forefinger and then the Trikol appear on Rubal's forefinger and started spinning.

Wow-what a weapon! Rubal said, Puneet

Dad, I have some doubts, may I ask? said Rubal

Yes-yes why not? said, Puneet

When I was about to go to school on the day of the Romana trip, you said " go and rock in Romana" so were you knowing this thing that I will get superpowers?

I was not sure whether you will pass the test or not, but I was sure that you will take part in it...

But how? Rubal interrupted

As when you take birth, Monk came to our home and told " Your child will be taken for the selection of superheroes"

Oh! and did you taken retirement yet?

No

Oh, so which superpower do you have? asked Rubal

Punnet said "I can throw 100s of arrows within a second"

Oh, how cool superpower you have!

And which power did Mom have? asked Rubal

She is having the power to throw flame. said, Sam

Oh wow!

Rubal, said Punnet, what's the name of your weapon?

'Trikol" said Rubal

After that Rubal's mom came there with Rubal's favourite cheeseburger and after eating it, Puneet said to Rubal " Wanna do some practice with me? "

Yes dad, why not

And after that Sam took Rubal to a secret place which Rubal had never seen.

Where we are? asked Rubal

This is a secret place where we use to do practise. said, Sam

There was a very giant ground and around it, there were a lot of commercial buildings which were now of no usage.

After that Puneet throw 100s of arrows toward Rubal while Rubal flung his " Trikol " towards the arrows, many arrows where fell because of the arrow which came out of " Trikol " and else the arrows were cut by the trikol.

Well done Rubal! Now I will not be going to throw hundreds of arrows nor 2 hundred arrows, I will throw thousands of arrows, Said, Puneet

What! it's impossible!

No, it is possible

After the Puneet throws thousands of arrows, While Rubal throws his trikol and moves it here and there but still a lot of arrows were left suddenly a bunch of arrows came near Rubal and at the time Rubal felt like that now he will be killed but at the last seconds he remembered about the bubble and he doesn't waste a second and made a defence bubble near him and as the arrows touched it all fall.

Oh, nice Rubal, said Puneet, at the last second you opened a defence bubble around you but remember that this bubble can handle limited things so it's not compulsory that every time you can be saved by the bubble.

Ok dad

After that, at night when Rubal was sleeping, he saw Monk in his dream and he was saying " from tomorrow you have to go to school, "I have teleported all the knowledge of 5th standard in your mind"

The next day...

Rubal went to school and he saw Blaze and Sherlin were also there and in their dreams too Monk came.

VI

Rescuing the Bank

That was a murky day and Rubal was enjoying his holiday, but suddenly Puneet came near Rubal and Puneet said: " Rub-Rubal you have to go to retrieval Kotak Mahindra Bank which is in our city!"

Wha-What has happened there? asked Rubal

There is some terrorist who has to commandeer the bank and a lot of people have been stuck in the bank, now you have to go there to save all of them and kill all the terrorists.

O-Ok dad, I am going and calling my friends too

Don't need to do that, said Puneet, they are also coming there and taking this secondary weapon which will also help you to fight the war and from this, you can fire flames and poison arrows.

But-but... said Rubal

And Puneet interrupted and said, " Ask me all your queries after completing this mission!"

After that Rubal reached near the bank and he suddenly glimpsed that he was wearing a red t-shirt but right now he was covered with a black suit and his face was also covered and when he saw Blaze and Sherlin both were too wearing a suit but that was a different one.

Rubal said to Sherlin and Blaze " We should first kill all the terrorists and then we will rescue the people", " No! said Blaze, we first enter the bank and then we will rescue people and kill the terrorists"

Your plan is very inadequate, I am going with my plan said Rubal and then he took out his "trikol" and throw it towards the window and it broke up and from where he can able to see a terrorist and the first terrorist was killed but after that, a blaring gun sound came from inside and the terrorist started shooting guns on the people inside the bank and they soon the gun bullets started coming out too.

Hey, what you did Rubal! now see what I will do said Blaze and after that, he fired a cannonball on the entrance gate and a big bomb blast happened there and more people die.

That's enough! what you both have done you know? said Sherlin, after that Sherlin uses her power and soon the bank started flying and then she moved it here and there and then she flung it on land again. And that's how all the terrorists die, after this, they all ran from there and soon cops entered the bank but after some time cops let know that 8 terrorists have been killed, 21 people also have been killed and many were injured.

When this news when came on television, Rubal was fearful and at that time Puneet came into the room and asked " How was the rescue operation?"

"fine" Rubal said

After that Rubal eat his dinner and went to bed. While sleeping he saw Monk in his dream " I am very regretful Monk" said Rubal. And suddenly Rubal saw Blaze and Sherlin in his dream and they are also regretting to Monk

Then suddenly Monk turned and said " Today what you have done!? You all have to kill evils, not the naive people, and when I gave you the task at the time you all have done teamwork that's why you won the war and this time also if you have done teamwork then also you shall surely win it, I am giving you last chance, performed well"

And suddenly Rubal's eyes opened and he saw that his mom and dad were sleeping.

oh, that was too horrific! Rubal murmured

And the next they all the 3 meets, and Rubal said " As monk told us the last night, we should do teamwork, so from the next time we will go with planning and also we will never be going to fight again for something silly like planning.

But, said Sherlin, we didn't notice about a thing

What's that asked both

Yesterday, when we all were going to rescue the bank, suddenly our clothes were changed into different suits, didn't you notice?

Oh, yea, I also noticed that thing but forgot to ask said Rubal

I think, said Blaze, this is because

Suddenly a man came there and interrupted blaze and said " On which topic discussion is going on? "

Oh, Sathya Uncle said Rubal

And then Blaze moved his head backwards and said " oh, dad! you are here"

Yes, what you all are discussing? asked Sathya

Uncle, we were discussing that when we were going to rescue the bank suddenly our whole body got covered in a suit and a mask came on our face, did you know why this all happened? Asked Sherlin

This is all because, when we also do rescue missions like you, these suits appeared on our body so no one can know us, said Sathya, but remember this was the first time that's why it automatically appeared on your body but from now whenever you will do some missions you will have to touch your head with forefinger and it will appear that.

Oh, wow! how cool is this, said Rubal

Yea, it's like we are ironman who wears his suit said, Blaze

Now a feeling coming like we are superhero said, Sherlin

Everyone Chuckle and,

Well, Uncle, did you give any secondary weapon to Blaze, asked Rubal, as my father also gave me a small weapon that looks like a pistol but from that fire and poising arrow comes out.

Yes, I gave Blaze a mini machine gun which is not too big and also its weight is light only 3kgs, this machine gun can shoot 100s of the bullet at a single time.

See, Rubal my secondary weapon is too strong said, Blaze

Yea, but my main weapon is stronger than yours said Rubal

Hey Blaze and Rubal! my secondary weapon is too strong and cute too. After that, she took out a small teddy, whose size was just 10 centimetres and she said " this looks like a teddy but it is having a button from which a small cannons ball comes out and it is not too big and It produces smoke from which no one can able to see anything for 3 minutes.

Yep, that's all sumptuous one, not only that all weapons are nice. Said Rubal

VII

The Training (second year)

After 2 months...

All the 3 reached Romana again, but this time there were more children there.

Who are you? asked Rubal

We have a training camp here said a child

But Simon the Monk teaches us said, Sherlin

He teaches us too, you all are just kids, you will not understand said a child

Oh, we are kids, I'm stronger!...

Just stop Blaze! Rubal interrupted

See your friend is also stopping you as he knows we are much stronger than you kids said the children

Hey! who are you first introduced yourself said Rubal

I'm Denial and who are you?

I'm Rubal

Oh, so you three are those who killed innocent people while rescuing the bank said Denial

After this everyone started giggling

Let me show my powers to this boy, Sherlin murmured in Blaze and Rubal's ear

Don't do this! said Rubal

No, you should do this, then they will let to know how powerful we are said, Blaze

And before Rubal can speak something, Sherlin uses her power and hang Denial in the sky

: Oh, aaa...!" let me come down you kids! said Denial

And then Sherlin throw him on land and everyone laughed and at that time Monk appears there.

At the time, everyone stops laughing and Denial stands up again.

I am teleporting you to Romana Gaur School, and after that, all the students were teleported to a school which was known as Romana Gaur School.

The School was too big and was looking like a castle and they all were in the auditorium and on stage Monk was standing for a few seconds everyone was looking here and there and then Monk clapped and said " You all are those, who have successfully passed your first year and in this year you will be divided into some teams and each team contain 17 students and the team which will perform the best, I will give it a present and also everyone is having 100points and it will also increase on some bases and remember they are very imported. So, this year we will study some more superpowers and how to fight the evils.

But-but how you will judge which team is best!? asked a child

For that, I will see how much you follow my rules, and how attentive you are in class, discipline said, Monk but for now, I am separating you into groups.

At that moment there were more the 50 students and that time, the hall was full of murmuring voices suddenly Monk clapped for attention and said: " There are 51 students and you all were divided into 3 groups, Monk took the name of the children's name one by one " So, Denial, Alex and Ron you are selected for " The Bolts" and everyone clapped for them and after that Monk took the name of Rubal at the time he was praying something and he came at the stage after that Monk took the name of Blaze and Sherlin and that's how one more group made and it was known as " The Thunders " and at that time all the three were very happy and again student started clapping, and the 3rd group was " The Splendid " and that's how 3 groups were divided and in every ground, there were 17 students.

Suddenly Bell rings...

It's your Weaponry class and it will be taken by Professor Abhishek Sir and in a while, a man came there who was Professor Abhishek, he was a long thin man with brown hair and he said " I'm Abhishek, your Weaponry professor and now all follow me" and after that, they all came out of the hall and there were some teleporting gates and it was in bluish and purplish colour which was looking like the galaxy and above the gates, there were written something.

There are seven gates, said Professor Abhishek, and their names are "Weaponry", this gate will teleport you to the class of weapons, the second gate is known as " Fortification" here you will learn " how to defend yourself from enemies", the third gate is known as "Pounce" here you will learn " how to attack your enemies with strategy" now the next gate will teleport you at " Main Area ", where you are having your bedroom, library, etc. The next gate will teleport you to the ground of Romana Gaur Castle, and the sixth gate is known as the " Restricted Chamber " as the name suggest that you are restricted here to enter, and if you will go there then it's impossible to return alive, so never try to entre in this gate... Now the last gate is the Sorcery gate where you will learn about black magic but not this year.

At the time everyone's eyes were at different-different gates but Rubal was the only one whose eyes were stuck on the restricted chamber gate and he said to Sherlin and Blaze " What can be there in the restricted chamber?"

I think there are some hostile powers or any secret thing can be there said, Sherlin

So now let's don't waste time and come with me to the " Weaponry " gate after that one by one everyone entered it and teleported to the Weaponry classroom. When it was the turn of Rubal, goosebumps were coming because of excitement and He was a little bit frightened too, he closed his eyes and ran towards the gate and at the next second when he opened his eyes he was that he was in a classroom and after he sat on the 2nd bench of the 1st row and after a while Blaze and Sherlin also came there, Blaze sat with Rubal while Sherlin sits on 2nd row at 2nd bench.

So, as you all have your primary and secondary weapons but today, I will tell you about a " fellow suit " which is black did anybody know about it? asked Abhishek

Suddenly Rubal raised his hand.

Oh, Mr Rubal, yes tell me

The suit is made for our disguise as when we are going to do any mission so no one will be able to know us and when we touch our head with forefinger the suit will cover us and when we wear it our speed also increased said Rubal

Well done Rubal said Abhishek and suddenly all the students of " The Thunder " started clapping, Rubal looked backwards towards Denial with show-off eyes and Denial bowed his head because of remorse.

Rubal, you spoke correct but there are some more things which I want to add. There will be a smartwatch in your hand permanently and it will tell you where you have to go for the mission also if you complete your mission you will unlock some achievements.

Sir, may you tell me which type of achievements we can unlock? asked Sherlin

Hm. You can unlock flying in the sky or have armour, etc. said Abhishek

But, Sherlin you can unlock this achievement but only in dreams. Denial makes a joke of Sherlin

Hey, Mr Denial! I am detecting your 10 points and also detecting 5 points of your team for your bad demeanour

No, I will see you after the class said Denial in an irate way to Sherlin

So, in tomorrow's class, I will teach you how to fly in the sky, said Abhishek

After that, all the students came out of the classroom and there was standing a teacher " I am Professor Bhist and I am your defence teacher" and after that suddenly all were teleported to the ground of Romana Gaur

Everyone was looking here and there like dumb as they don't know anything, and Rubal said to Blaze " What these professors are doing! we just put out our leg from class and a professor appears and said "hello my name is this" and then he teleported."

Blaze laughed and said, " Yes, you are correct, I think they have eaten anything from which they are doing this all!"

After that, Rubal moved forward and said " Professor how did you do this!?"

I will teach you it in the 3rd year, so in today's class we are going to learn how to defend ourselves and so today we will go to do practise will sward.

But-But Professor I want to ask that if we have superpowers, said Sherlin, then why we are fighting with a sword

Because if one day, you need to fight with any weapon which doesn't have a superpower then what will happen? that's why we will practise with sward today.

I think this professor doesn't even know how to teach; Blaze whispered into Rubal's eyes.

Hey, what you both are whispering!? asked Professor Bhist

Ah...Ah... Sir Rubal was saying that you don't know how to teach said Blaze

Wha-What! said Rubal and was looking with his torn eyes.

Oh, then you Mr Rubal come here and teach me how should I teach students said Bhist

Si-Sir I-I

Nothing! Just come here and teach us!

Blaze, did Rubal say this thing? asked Sherlin in Blaze's ear

I said this thing but in fear, I took the name of Rubal

Wow! what a dupe you are, are you mad? don't you know that now Rubal is in big trouble! shrieked Sherlin

Quit busting my chops now! shouted Blaze

Meanwhile, Rubal said " I don't have anything to teach sir"

Oh, now you have to do 1 v 1 against me, and if you lose, I will give you a very dangerous punishment said, Professor

And after that Professor took out a big Hammer and at the time Rubal's legs were shaking he took out his Trikol and after that Professor throw his hammer at 100km/s speed and Rubal closed and eyes and his hands were shaking and suddenly a loud sound came and he opened his eyes and he saw that Professor's hammer was broken up in pieces and Rubal don't able to understand how it broke up.

At that time Bhist's eyes and face turned red and his teeth grinding.

What! you broke my favourite hammer now you will not be going to be safe! and after that, 100 arrows came there and Professor throws them toward Rubal Rubal bravely cut all of them as he did practice this with his father.

How! ho-how di... did you do that! said, Professor.

Everyone was enjoying the fight else Rubal and everyone's eyes were stuck on Professor Bhist, that now what he will be going to do?

Professor Bhist closed his eyes, and started murmuring something, I few seconds a big sword appears in Professor's hands

O My God, cried Blaze, a giant sword, what do you think how much length this sword can have? he asked Sherlin

But no reply came from Sherlin's sides.

Blaze moved his hand in front of Sherlin's face and suddenly her eyes blinked.

What happened to you? asked Blaze

Nothing! she shouted, you are watching the sword length, don't you think what Professor will be going to do with this sword!?

And in the next second, Professor's sword colour changes to blue and, then he hit his sword on the ground and in a second Rubal's leg got frozen by ice.

Ah. Ah... it's too chilly, off... Rubal cried

After that Bhist laughed and suddenly his sword colour changed to red and he again hit it on the ground and in the next second the ground started shrinking and breaking up from the middle and the ground also started catching fire and it started coming towards Rubal.

Rubal started shouting and he was trying to move but sadly he can't.

At that time, Professor and Denial were laughing and Sherlin took out her gulps hurriedly.

But what's that?

Suddenly all fire got disappeared and the broken land again started moving and joined again.

Professor looked here and there in anger and he saw Simon the Monk was there and he said " Professor what had happened to you!? don't you know the rules of Romana Gaur School!?

Sir, he said that I don't know how to teach students, said Bhist

That's a very wrong thing but Bhist remember never again to do these things! said Monk

Suddenly children started shouting " Rubal has fainted because of ice!"

Oh, no, and then Monk teleported him to the hospital of Romana Gaur.

THE NEXT DAY...

Rubal's eyes blinked and he murmured " Professor...Professor, I don-don't speak anything bad for you "

Yea. Yea we know that Rubal said, Sherlin

After that Rubal's eyes opened properly and he saw on his left side that Blaze and Sherlin were shitting and on his right side a doctor and professor Bhist was sitting.

I-I am very sorry, Rubal said Bhist

Sir-Sir that's fine said Rubal, but may you tell me why I fainted?

You fainted because the frozen ice temperature was -500degrees Celsius and god knows how you survived, I was worried because maximum of the people can't bear this and they died... Rubal you were lucky.

Not that exactly...

Everyone turned their head and Monk was standing.

He was able to bear it because he is having god-gifted power. said Monk

What god-gifted power! cried everyone at once

Yes, Rubal, I want to ask that did you ever try to remove your ring in which a purple stone is there from your figure?, asked Monk

Yes, I tried it many times but can't able to remove it, and not only me, my mom and dad also tried this thing but this ring is in my hand from my birth.

And you never told this thing to me! to your best friend! cried, Blaze

Blaze, first make your memories strong, then talk to me! I have already told this thing to you and you lied to Professor Bhist that I said that " Professor don't even know how to teach! " and because of this today I am lying in bed!

Wh... What! It was you, Blaze! shouted Professor

Um...Ah...N... Blaze murmured

Leave it for now, you all can discuss it later, said Sherlin, let me first listen to what Monk is saying

Hm..., After that Monk moved forward and pointed to Rubal's ring and said " This is not an ordinary ring this is a god-gifted ring and because of this ring you survived -500-degree Celsius temperature and it will help you to fight WWV again, said Monk

Who is WWS? asked Rubal

WhiteWash Venom said, Sherlin

Sherlin doesn't take his full name only says " WWV " said Monk

But why? we can't speak his name asked Blaze

Because if you take his name then it is believed that he will come into your dream and make become a nightmare and will pester your mind said, Monk

Like these days went on...

One day, when Rubal, Blaze and Sherlin were roaming here and there in the school, they saw a cat coming near them, The cat was very different from other cats, it was red, and her eyes were whole black, and her nails were sharp as a knife and the most shocking thing was that from her right side both legs only she was moving but the left side legs were not working and it was looking like she was having polio in one side, while here right side ear was straight ear while left side one was fallen off and this same was with her moustache, her right side-eye was opened and was blinking while left side-eye was closed, and it was looking like her half body was working and half is not.

But when Rubal saw that cat suddenly he started feeling pain in his right-hand figure in which he was wearing the ring and purple stone started shining and a shadow reflected on the nearby wall and there was a half-man and something else which Rubal can't able to understand, the cat was continuously watching Rubal only.

Ahh...Ahhh... it's paining a lot, Rubal cried

In the next second Denial and his one friend came there and said " Vonspite, where you are going? come here"

I think we shall take him to the doctor said, Sherlin

Y-yes Blaze said

After that, when Doctor checked it, she said " Nothing had happened to you "

N-No, the pain was too much, said Rubal, I think we shall go to Monk and tell him about the problem.

Yes, tell me the problem, a voice came from the back

Rubal moved his head backwards and said "Mo-monk, how do you know that I was talking about you? "

Monk chuckled and said " I am a soul, and I roam here and there and suddenly I hear Monk from your mouth so I came here. So, tell me the problem

After this, Rubal told everything.

Hmm... Someone has tried to kill you and the ring protects you and that's why you were feeling pain

Bu-but who will try to kill me... said Rubal shockingly as there was no one only me, Sherlin and Blaze.

No there was a cat also said, Sherlin

But how can a cat kill me, said Rubal

Whose cat was that? asked Monk

When we are about to come here, I saw that Denial was saying " Where are you going Vonspite? ", I mean that the cat is of Denial

Oh okay, give me some time I will tell you who tried to kill you said, Monk

In Evening

Rubal, Blaze and Sherlin were going towards their bedroom and while talking Rubal saw Denial going somewhere.

Hey, see Denial is going somewhere said Rubal

Rubal, Denial is also going to his bedroom only. said Blaze

Bu-But the way to go to the bedroom is on the left side but He's going upwards said Rubal

Yes, Rubal is saying accurate, Blaze, upwards there is only a restricted chamber.

Let's chase him, said Rubal

After that they started chasing Denial, while chasing, suddenly Blaze stopped and sneezed.

And then Denial stopped and when he was almost about to turn, Sherlin took out her teddy and spread out smoke and all the 3 hides near about.

After some seconds, Rubal stand up and move forward and saw that there was no one, he calls Blaze and Sherlin to come out.

They move forward and after a while, they saw Denial with his cat and Professor Abhishek who was breaking that wall of the restricted chamber and there was a huge gate.

Here you are, I watched you! Denial

What are you doing here? Asked Denial

The same question for you, said, Blaze

Go to your bedroom, what are you doing here! Go now! Abhishek Shouted

Let's go to Monk's room and tell him about this thing, Blaze murmured in Rubal's ear.

Professor! He will tell the wrong thing to Monk, stop them! Denial cried

But before Professor can do something, Sherlin spread smoke everywhere and the 3 ran towards Monk's room behind them Abhishek and Denial also started running.

Monk-Monk, Rubal said while taking a deep breath

Yes, what happens?

And in the next second Denial and Abhishek also reached there.

What you all are doing here? Monk asked

Monk, Denial... Rubal speak while taking a long breath

Suddenly Monk saw Denial taking out his sword and within the next second Monk did magic and the sword started flying and Monk said " I didn't accept this from you that you will be going to kill him "

Yes, Rubal continue said, Monk

Yes, I was saying that I saw Denial and Professor Abhishek at a restricted chamber where they were doing something, said Rubal

Oh, so what you both were doing there? Monk asked

Professor, Denial said that his cat got into the restricted chamber and she left her teddy there. said, Professor Abhishek

No, Monk, he is lying! how can my cat can get into the chamber and Professor Abhishek only told me that if you enter into the chamber then you can't return alive, so if my cat gets into the chamber so did you think she can return?... said Denial

No-No, Abhishek interrupted, you said to me that there is a bit of space between the gate and the floor that's why she got inside.

Wait Abhishek, let me first hear what Denial is saying, cried the monk

Yes, Monk, actually Professor Abhishek said " Denial I want to show you something, it's very secret and I came with Professor and now he is lying. said Denial

No-No Professor... Abhishek said

Stop! Abhishek, if it is like that then why do you take out your sword Denial? Monk asked

Umm... Because Professor murmured in my ear to do that so, said Denial

Wait, come with me to the restricted chamber and Abhishek broke the wall and said, Monk

Ok Professor

After that Rubal, Blaze, Sherlin, Denial, Monk and Abhishek go there.

Then Abhishek opened his hands and a blue ring started rotating around Abhishek at the time Rubal, Blaze, Sherlin and Denial's eyes teared up after that Abhishek moved his hands towards the restricted chamber wall and that broke up within a second and when everyone saw what was there, everyone sweat starts coming out accept Monk and Abhishek leg started shrinking and Monk moved towards Abhishek and said " You have killed a student and you lied me! "

No-No Professor not like that said Abhishek

You Cheater, I will kill you...

And before Monk could able to do anything suddenly Professor Abhishek spread smoke everywhere and disappeared from there

After that students started getting scared of professors and their moms and dad started protesting against the school.

The Next Day

Rubal and Sherlin were talking to Professor Bhist and suddenly a voice came " Rubal-Rubal, see what I found" and that voice was of Blaze and he came there with a newspaper in his hand and he said, " see what is written in this!"

What's there? asked Professor Bhist

The news came from " The Times of India " which tell about the superhero's news and in that there was written that...

Death of 4 students in 3 schools!Yesterday 4 murder cases came in 3 schools and 3 teachers got fired from their jobs for killing students, this is a very disappointing thing, the Schools from where these murder cases come are - Romana Gaur, Velenska Gaur and The Sandfrancis Gaur School, 1 murder case found in Romana Gaur and One found in Velenska Gaur and 2 found in Sandfrancis Gaur School.While "Simon The Monk" the Headmaster of Romana Gaur School and said that " We have changed some policy of the school and also I have made some invisible traps which will help to find the people who will try to kill our pupils"And the "Prison of Gaur" is finding Abhishek who was the Professor of Romana Gaur and escaped on the last day.

Hmm... I never think that Abhishek can do this type of thing said Professor Bhist

I think Abhishek planned to kill students one by one said Rubal

No... this thing I'm not able to understand is that for the last 20 years he is teaching in this school and not only that he studied in this school only but if it was his plan then why he did do this thing yesterday only... god knows said

Professor Bhist

Now only 50 students are left in this school. said Blaze

No, there are more than 600 students! cried Bhist

What! but there were 51 only said Rubal

This year 51 more students join this school and else students are older one said Bhist

At Night...

When everyone was sleeping suddenly Rubal woke up and he was taking a long breath

Wh-What happen Rubal? Blaze asked

No-nothing that was just a nightmare. said Rubal

Oh, now sleep because tomorrow is our last day in school and after that Diwali breaks!

After that in the morning, Rubal woke up and he saw no one was in the room, he came out of the room and can't able to see anyone! he went everywhere and still, he can't able to find anyone, suddenly he saw a student going somewhere.

Hey-hey, hello Rubal cried

But that student was walking continuously without giving any answer and then Rubal chased that student after a minute the student and Rubal came to the ground of the school, and he saw a lot of students standing there.

Rubal moved forward and saw everyone was silent and their head were down.

Rubal entered into the bunch of students and moved forward and forward and in a while, he saw Blaze and Sherlin there standing.

Blaze, Sherlin, why everyone is here what happened!? asked Rubal

But no reply came from their side and Sherlin and Blaze moved their figure forward, then Rubal moved forward and saw Monk and when he saw the ground, he became stunned and there were lying Rubal's mom and dad.

What... what had happened to them, Monk? asked Rubal while taking a long breath

They are no more in this world said Monk in a miserable voice

No! this can't happen and Rubal started crying after that Blaze and Sherlin came there and said " Rubal control yourself"

Bu-But who had kill-Killed them? Rubal said while crying

"WWS," said Monk

Suddenly Rubal's face turned red and said " WhiteWash Venom! "

Don't take his name said a student

Why am I will not going to take his name, he killed my mom and dad, I will be going to kill him! but ho-how my mom and dad lying here.

Today, I let to know that 2 days before WWS came your Mom and dad dream and he said " come to Lakshadweep Island or I will kill your son" but they ignore it and the next day in the morning a bomb blast was there at their home terrace and a paper was left there and on that, there was written if you don't come then I will kill your son now! " and after that, they go to Lakshadweep and there was standing WWS but he was half of a human and he attacked at your mom and dad and they also attacked at him but they lose and died as WWS was too strong.

At night this same dream came to me and they were fighting WWV but in fear, I woke up and can't able to see what happened next. Bu-but why was he killed by Mom and dad? asked Rubal

Because if he killed 50% of the world's superheroes and get all the five-ring and one of them is in your figure then he will become immortal. said Monk

And till now he has killed 7% of the world's superheroes! said, Sherlin

Leave that all, firstly Monk please tell me who is WWS and from where he is? why he is half of a human? and why he is too strong?

Ok now I will tell you the story of "WhiteWash Venom"

VIII

Story of WhiteWash Venom

300 years ago, on a planet known as GeForce 19, there were 4 brothers and their dream was to rule the whole universe for that they merged themself. said Monk

What! they merged themselves! cried, Sherlin

Yes, they were also superheroes like you all and with their powers, they merge themselves after merging themselves, a man formed which was known as WhiteWash Venom Spite...

Blaze interrupted and said " What! too long a name, if I merge mine, mom and dad's names then also it is small than his name! Blaze chuckle

Yes, because White, Wash, Venom and Spite are the names of the brothers and they merge their names. said Monk

At that time, Rubal was not speaking anything and was continuously listening.

So, after that, they became too strong and now if anyone wants to kill them then they have to kill them 4 times after that WhiteWash Venom can die.

After that, they aimed to kill 5 lords because after killing them WWS will be got the stones and from this, he can control the whole world.

The lords were having different-different powers, The red lord was having the power to change its appearance and the second lord was Blue Lord who was having the power to control someone's mind while the third lord was the Black lord who was having the power to teleport anywhere, the 4th lord was Yellow lord who was having the power to watch future, present and past of anyplace while the last lord which was knowns as Purple lord was having the power to time travel. And if anyone got all these stones and killed 50% of the superheroes then he or she will be immortal. And this thing Whitewash Venom wants.

For that, he fight with the Red and Black lords and in that, the Red and Black gods got defeated and Whitewash Venom got 2 stones after this when the rest of 3 lords saw this they understood that they can't fight WWV and that's why they send these stones on earth at random places and one of that stone Rubal had and Rubal your stone is very important as you can do time travel from this.

Really! but how can I do it!? asked Rubal

This thing I don't know how it can possible but yes, it is possible said Monk

So, that's why WWS is finding all the people who are having these stones and killing superheroes so that he can be immortal but remember Rubal one-day WWV will surely attack you to take that stone and at that time you have to fight against him bravely.

And if you talk about why WWV is half then he is because when he comes on earth he becomes 1 fourth of a human but now he is half because he has taken 2 stones and killed 7% of superheroes, so if he killed more superheroes and taken more stones then he will look like a human.

Bu-but I am not even too much power that I can fight him said Rubal

Yes, that's why you are in this school, so this was the story of WWV

After that, everyone gives tribute to Rubal's mom and dad for their braveness.

The Next day, was Diwali and the school was closed for the next 10 days, Rubal started staying at Blaze's home.

IX

Monster's attack on the city

That was a chilly day,

Rubal was very sad and was sitting in the corner of Blaze's bedroom.

At that time Sherlin was also there at Blaze's home.

When they saw Rubal, they sit near Rubal and said " What happened Rubal?

Nothing, said Rubal in a slow voice

After that Blaze and Sherlin went out of the room and Blaze told his father Sathya about Rubal

Sathya came into Blaze's room and said to Rubal " come here Rubal, I have something for you! "

After that, they all took Rubal to the drawing-room and there was a cake, pizza and much more!

Wow! but when did you bring this all? asked Rubal

I did magic! said Sathya

Rubal, Blaze and Sherlin started doing a party; and Blaze said " let's watch some news" after that when he switched on the news, he saw that there are some aliens had attacked the city!

Hey, what! Aliens have attacked the city! Said Sherlin

We have to save the city now! said Rubal

And after that, they touch their head and the suit covers them.

A watch came into their hands and they saw that the city is 30 kilometres!

After that wings came out and they all started flying in the sky and soon they reached the city within 3miniiutes

Wa-What! Did we reach the city? How said Rubal

Let's don't talk about that and focus on our mission said, Blaze

Okok said Rubal

There they saw that 2 giant monsters were demolishing the city

Hey, stop monsters! said Rubal. The monster was blue and green and their eyes were big and their legs and hands were also big.

They moved their heads downwards and he laughed, ha-ha kids have come to stop me

Oh, said Blaze, and then he took out his wiper and shoot a cannon on the monster's tummy and he said: " ouch ouch... you kid!"

It was just 1% of my whole power, and it damages you a lot said, Blaze

I will never forgive you and then the monster yanks out a tree and throw it at Blaze.

No way and Rubal took out his " trikol" and made a defence bubble towards Blaze and the tree falls to the ground

Thanks, Rubal, said, Blaze

Of... Said the other monster and then he opens his mouth and throw fire toward Rubal, but that fire paused and it return towards monster 2 and hit on his hand and it started burning, he fled from there and ran nearby, and this was all because of Sherlin

I am going towards the monster 2, said Rubal, till then you both beat monster 1

After that...

Sherlin used her power and fly Monster 1 in the air and then she throws it onto the land again after that Blaze throw his most powerful cannon at the monster and it blast into his hand and now, he was left with only one hand.

At that time, public people were running here and there.

" ah ah ouch" Monster 1 murmured

Meanwhile, Rubal reached near monster 2

I think you what that you will be dead, that's why you came here and after that, he throws arrows at Rubal and Rubal cut all of them with his trikol and then throw arrows from trikol and the poisons arrow hit at the monster and he fell at the ground but in a minute he again wakes up and throws cannonball on Rubal and Rubal made the defence bubble and started laughing but Monster was continuously throwing it and soon Rubal was able to see cracks on the bubble and understood that it can't handle much. He moved from there and took out his secondary weapon and started throwing flame on the monster after that he throw the trikol at the Monster and firstly he cut the monster into 2 parts and that's how he died.

While Blaze and Sherlin were continuously attacking the monster and in end, Sherlin took him at 4500m in the air and then throwback on land when he was falling from the sky he started burning and Blaze then shoots a cannonball and he died.

That's how the mission got successfully

Yeee... We did that said Sherlin

And suddenly a throng of people started shouting " Long live Black Hero. Long live Black Hero" and people started coming towards them for their interview.

We shall go now, all we all will be divulged said Rubal

Sherlin use your teddy and spread smoke so that we can run easily from here

After that, Sherlin throw fog every, and they all ran

After that, the 3 go again to Blaze's home and continue their party.

X

Returning to School

The holidays were about to end only 3 days were left!

That was a frozen day, Rubal and Blaze were practising together of their superpowers and after that Blaze and Rubal did a 1V1 and in that Blaze took out his machine gun and shoot a lot of bullets but Rubal can't able to defend himself and a lot of bullets stuck at Rubal's body and he said " Please! Blaze stop this! it is hurting! "

Blaze stopped his machine gun and said " don't you even be able to bear these bullets!? Blaze chuckled and said " you are having this ring then, why you are feeling pain? "

Blaze! if I am having a ring that doesn't mean that it will not be going to hurt me! said Rubal

Oh, if it is like that, then why you were not able to defend my bullets? didn't your dad tell you how to defend?! opps you don't even have a dad! said, Blaze

Suddenly Rubal's face turned red and moved forward toward Blaze and hold Blaze's shirt collar and said " don't ever again say this thing! "

Blaze push Rubal and said " I can and I will! you stay in my home ok, be happy about that only! "

After that Rubal ran from there and reached Blaze's house he went into his room and locked the door.

Suddenly Rubal's room started shrinking and a man came there!

He was wearing a black cloak and his eyes were red with a sneer.

Who-Who are you! Rubal asked

Ha-Ha-Ha I am Amon and I the right hand of WWVS! I am here to take your ring!

As Rubal listened to this, Rubal put his hand into the pocket and at that time Rubal's leg started shrinking as in the pocket there was no weapon, suddenly he remembered that " he left his trikol at the playground where He and Blaze were doing practice.

And after that Amon opened his hand and blue energy started rotating near his right hand.

Suddenly a thing hits Rubal's mind and he opened his forefinger and he closed his eyes and started murmuring " please trikol, please come"

And the next second Amon throws that blue energy towards Rubal and what's that! suddenly Rubal's room window glass broke up and trikol entered in this room and while coming towards Rubal forefinger trikol touched that blue energy and that blue energy reflected towards Amon and the next second Amon blowdown and that Blue energy touched the wall and in a second a small part of the wall got melted.

Oh no! said Amon and he got disappeared

At that time knock...knock sound came at Rubal's door and a sound comes " What had happed Rubal?! just open the door!" said Blaze's mother "Gayatri"

After that, Rubal opened the gate.

Sathya and Gayatri came into the room and saw that the window was broken, while a small part of the wall was melted near the window.

How did this all happen?! Rubal asked Sathya

But Rubal didn't give any answer

At that, Blaze came there and said " leave dad, he will not going to answer because he has done this all.

"No! I didn't"say Rubal

Oh, then who did this? asked Blaze

"Amon," said Rubal

What! The right hand of WWV said Sathya

Why did he come here? tell Rubal asked Gayatri

He said that " I am here to take your stone " and after that, he was just about to attack and my trikol came by breaking this window "

Mom and dad, this is all just fake, this can't even happen! said Blaze, actually today he started arguing with me and I defeat him in 1V1 and that's why he was angry and do this all said Blaze

No! you are lying! you started the argument and you came to my dad! You are my best friend that's why I leave you said Rubal

Now both of you stop said Sathya

Listen, Blaze, you should not talk to Rubal like this, now say sorry to him and Rubal hug him said Sathya

Umm... Blaze murmured

And he looked around and saw everyone's eyes were staring at Blaze only!

Blaze said " I-I am So-Sorry "

And at that time a small grin came to Rubal's face and they both hug each other!

After 3 days...

All again reached Romana Gaur School

All again reached Romana Gaur School, When Rubal and Blaze were going towards their bedroom with their luggage, they saw Sherlin there!

Hello! Sherlin, said Blaze

At that same time, Sherlin turned toward Blaze and Rubal, her face was red and was looking like she was very angry. Sher didn't give any response and she again turned towards the bedroom area.

What! She ignored us! Said Blaze

By the way, she ignored you not me, I don't even say anything to her. Said Rubal

Leave that, the question arises why she is not replying!? Asked Blaze

After that Rubal think for a while and said "I think, we should ask her "

After this, Rubal and Blaze come into the bedroom and said at once "Why you are not giving any answer?! "

I will never talk to you both! Cried, Sherlin

Bu-But why? Asked Rubal

What we have done? Asked Blaze

We were having a 10 days holiday and you don't even come to my home for once! Cried, Sherlin

Umm... Blaze murmured

Acutely, on holiday we were doing research said Rubal

Really!? If it is like that then tell me which research you both were doing? Asked Sherlin

"Hmm... we were finding the location of "WWV" and we were too busy that we forgot to come to your home," said Rubal

Oh, so where he is? Asked Sherlin

"WWV" is in disguise as Denial cat. said Rubal

After listening to this, Sherlin's face becomes normal and Both Blaze and Sherlin asked at once "How do you know that and what's the prove?!"

What! You were doing research with Rubal then why you are asking this? Asked Sherlin

Acutely, I give motivation to Rubal and he does research, said Blaze

Leave that, said Rubal "I want to tell you that I have found some evidence that the cat is "WWV" only. First of all, the day a student died in our school, we saw Denial can for the first time, and as you know that before these holidays, there was not a single holiday we got and as we know that we can't get out of school till then there are holiday"

Blaze and Sherlin's eyes stared at Rubal and they were listening very carefully, and thank god that Blaze didn't sneeze yet.

Ahhh...chuuuuuuuuu, Blaze sneezed

Oh no! again Blaze said, Sherlin

What can do? Tell me, I can't control this, Blaze said in a crying Manner

Yea, Sherlin, it's not the fault of Blaze, he can't even able to control it! Said Rubal

Oh ok, now please continue said, Sherlin

Yea, said Rubal, "So when we can't get out of the school then from where did Denial get the cat?"

Yea Rubal, I agree with this, but I think Professor Abhishek and Denial did teamwork but when they both were caught and Denial lied and Professor Abhishek was out of the school. Said Blaze, "I am having a Paranoid on Denial only"

Hmm..., You are correct Blaze, and also you remembered that when I saw that cat, I started feeling pain! I think “WWV” tried to kill me but I got saved because of the ring. Said Rubal

Not only this, said Sherlin, “don’t you remember when Rubal started feeling pain, a shadow appeared on the wall and when Rubal saw the dream that his mother and father are fighting with someone, don’t you saw a half-man who was covered with fire and that same man we saw on the wall”

Rubal grinned and said “Sherlin you stool my point; I was just about to say the same thing”

“Now, in my opinion, we should pursue Denial for the whole day”, said Blaze, “Hope we could find something”

Wow, Blaze, what had happened to you today, earlier you were a foolish guy and today... said Sherlin

What do you mean? I am a foolish or a smart one? Asked Blaze

Both! Sherlin chuckle

After that they came out of the Bedroom and Blaze murmured in Rubal’s ear, “We don’t even do any research then how you were able to know these things?”

Blaze, said Rubal, “I am not a couch potato like you! in the night I use to do research”

After that, they started finding Denial and after almost 20 minutes they found Denial who was talking to his friends and his cat was also there. For the whole day, Rubal, Blaze and Sherlin chase Denial, but can’t able to find anything.

Ahh... we can’t find anything today said, Blaze

Now, I am peeved, said Sherlin, we did a laborious today, but in end... can’t able to find anything!

Yea, now I am feeling drowsy, I am going to the bedroom said Rubal

The Next day

Let's chase Denial! Cried Rubal

No, today, I am fatigued, I will not be going to chase him said, Blaze

Same here said, Sherlin

Ok then, let's do furlough today said Rubal

In Afternoon

Rubal was wandering around the ground of Romana Gaur School, the next seconds he saw that Denial was going somewhere and Rubal started chasing Denial and after a while, Rubal saw that Denial is going towards the main gate of Romana Gaur School and when Rubal saw the gate he was astonished that the gate was opened and after that Rubal run hastily and hastily towards Blaze and Sherlin and told everything to them.

What! The main gate is open, how it is possible! Cried Blaze

I think this all is done by "WWV", let's don't fritter time and let's chase Denial said Rubal

And after that all the 3 reached the gate and the gate was still open, they all came out of the school and in front there was a large forest and they saw Denial was going inside the forest only!

They all again started chasing Denial and when they were chasing Denial suddenly, he got disappeared somewhere.

Where had he gone? Asked Rubal

He got disappeared! Cried, Sherlin

Suddenly Rubal felt like he was pushed by someone and Rubal fall to the ground, the next second, he turned and found that Blaze has pushed him!

Wh-What are you doing Blaze! Shrieked Rubal

Hahahaha, I will obliterate you! Blaze laughed

Are you mad?! What you are doing! Said Rubal

After that, Blaze took out his wiper and shoot a cannonball toward Rubal and the next second Rubal jumped towards the left side and cried “Sherlin stop Blaze! “

But no reply came from Sherlin’s side, she was just staring at Rubal

After that Rubal dawned, that something had happened to Sherlin and Blaze

After that Rubal took out his “trikol” and cut the cannonball that was thrown by Blaze

Sherlin, do your work or we shall lose! Cried Blaze

Suddenly, Rubal started flying in the sky and when he looked downwards, he saw that “Sherlin was using here gulps”

Now, you can kill him, I have paused him said, Sherlin

After that Blaze aims at Rubal and at that time Rubal can’t able to move.

Blaze! Sherlin! What you both are doing! Let me come down! Said Rubal

But they both ignore it and Blaze was ready with his wiper to kill Rubal at that time Rubal closed his eyes as he was knowing that he will be going to die now.

Suddenly a sound came from somewhere and Rubal saw that Blaze was falling to the ground and there was standing Professor Abhishek, who was using his superpowers.

You Abhishek! Cried, Sherlin

After that, red energy started rotating around Professor Abhishek's right hand and he throw it towards Sherlin and she all fell to the ground!

As Sherlin fell to the ground, Rubal started falling "Ahhh..." Rubal screamed

And the next second Abhishek catch Rubal

After that Rubal was about to say something but Abhishek said "we don't have time for talking right now"

Then Blaze and Sherlin stand again and Blaze said "I am the right hand of "WWV" named Amon

Then Sherlin said "I am the left hand of "WWV" named Ramon

What! Do you both want! Said Rubal

We need your ring! said both at once, after that they came in their real form

After that Amon took out his hammer and Ramon took out his "Axeman" which was looking like an axe but was much bigger than the normal axe and sharper.

After this, Rubal took out his trikol and Abhishek took out his sword.

They all started fighting...

Ramon started fighting Abhishek and Amon started fighting Rubal

As Amon throws his hammer toward Rubal, Rubal cut the hammer bravely

You bloody guy, said Amon and after that, blue energy started forming around Amon's hands and he throw it towards Rubal, and the next Rubal bow down and the blueish energy hit a tree and destroyed it.

After that Rubal throw his trikol toward Amon and the Trikol cuts Amon's right hand!

Now say to yourself "Right hand of WWV! " said Rubal

While Abhishek and Ramon were fighting and the fight was too dangerous! They both were attacking each other but after some time Abhishek broke Ramon's Axeman by his sword and both started running towards the Romana Gaur School.

Rubble and Professor Abhishek started chasing both of them.

Both Amon and Roman went near a restricted area and the next second Abhishek and Rubal also reached there, but Amon and Roman started murmuring something and they both got disappeared and when they disappeared, a paper was lying on the floor, the paper was too big but as Abhishek opened the paper there was nothing written.

Shit! We can't able to catch them said Abhishek

Professor-Professor! What is happening on, I am not able to understand! Cried Rubal, "Why did you save me?"

Rubal, let me tell you everything, that day when, Professor Simon, throw me out of school, I hide in the forest of Romana Gaur and I didn't do anything! Denial lied and

Professor believed him! I didn't kill that student but still, everyone started saying me a murderer and today when I was in the forest, I heard the sound of a cannonball and that's why I ran towards you and saw all this thing.

Oh, I am sorry, I told the wrong thing about you to Monk

No, that's fine, right now we have to save your friends Blaze and Sherlin said, Professor Abhishek

Bu-But where we will find them? Asked Rubal

In the next second, Rubal and Abhishek's eyes stared at the big paper which is in Abhishek's hand.

There is something for sure in this paper said Abhishek

Yes, but we can't able to see anything said Rubal

Abhishek think for a while and said "I think someone has done black magic on this paper and that's why we can't able to see what is written on it"

So, do you know how to break this black magic? Asked Rubal

No, I don't but yes professor Mradu knows how to break the black magic spell. Said, professor Abhishek

Who is this professor? I never heard her name? asked Rubal

She teaches about Black magic and from next year you will also learn Blackmagic from her only. Said Abhishek

After that Rubal and Abhishek went to Professor Mradu's room

When Professor Mradu saw Professor Abhishek she said "from where did you come?"

After that Abhishek told all the things to Professor Mradu

Oh okay, so what help do you both need?

Rubal pointed toward the paper which was in Abhishek's hand and said "we need to know what is written in this paper"

Oh, just wait said Professor Mradu

After that, Professor Mradu took the paper and started murmuring something and soon all the letters appear on the paper.

There is written “The way to come in “SHQOWWV” is by murmuring a magical line near restricted chamber which you will found at “Reangle” in Romana Gaur,” said Professor Mradu

Where is Reangle? Asked Professor Abhishek and Rubal at once

Here is written"inside the Romana Gaur" it means the magic line is in the school only...

But at Reangle, I never heard this name. Rubal interrupted

There should be a place named Reangle but who can know this? Asked Professor Abhishek

Only, Monk knows that because he has only made this school. Said Rubal

Then you should go and ask Monk said Professor Mradu

But Rubal remember don’t take my name or don’t say that I need to save my friends because if you said this then Monk will not let us go there. Said Abhishek

Ok, said Rubal, I will make an excuse

After that Rubal went to Monk’s Room and asked Monk “Monk I want to know where is “Reangle” located in this school?”

Well, why you are asking me? Asked Monk

Um... because I was reading about the history of Romana Gaur and I found a word named “Reangle” in a book. Said Rubal

Monk grinned and said “Reangle, is the cemetery, where there are coffins of the superheroes who are dead and 70 years before it was known as Reangle”

After that Rubal ran hastily towards Professor Mradu room's and told them about this thing.

Nice, let's go there and find the magic line said, Professor Abhishek

After that, they all went to Reangle

Now where we will find that magic line asked Rubal

In my opinion, the magic line can be in the coffin. Said Professor Mradu

After that, Abhishek said "I am sorry, but I have to do this and after that, he took out something which Rubal was not able to understand and after that the land started shrinking.

Wh-What is happening!? Rubal asked

And after that, all the coffins came out from the ground.

Rubal and Professor Mradu started to find that magical line and till then, Abhishek was holding these coffins.

After that both Rubal and Professor Mradu started finding the magical line and when Rubal was finding the magical line he saw his dad's coffin, suddenly tears came out of Rubal's eyes and he saw something written on it and when he read it carefully then he saw there was written " Yesterday was History, Tomorrow is Mystery and today is WhiteWash Venom Spite"

Professor-Professor I founded the line!

Where did you find that? asked Professor Mradu

But no reply came from Rubal's side and he said "Professor Abhishek now you can put the coffins in their right place.

After that, they all went into Restricted Chamber and Rubal said "we don't even realize a thing!" said Rubal

What's that? Asked both at once

That when we murmur this Magical line then we will reach "HQOWWV" said Rubal, now what is the full form of this place?

When we will speak that magical line automatically, we will reach there. said Professor Mradu

After that, all the 3 murmured the magical line and after 3 seconds Rubal opened his eyes and he found himself somewhere which was looking like a room made up of red bricks when Rubal moved his head left and right and he saw Professor Abhishek and Mradu were also there, the next second he saw a big cage in which Blaze and Sherlin were there!

Blaze! Sherlin! How do you go there? Asked Rubal

Oh, Rubal! Cried both, they were sedated up and locked up in this cage.

Who? Asked Rubal, sedation you?

I and Roman did that said someone

Oh, Amen and Roman said Abhishek

After that Rubal saw Denial was also there with his cat.

You liar Denial! Cried Rubal

After that Denial put his cat on the ground and the cat started moving with only 2 legs on the right side.

And within 5 seconds that cat changes into Whitewash Venom Spite!

He was half just half of a person! Everywhere fire was burning and he laugh and said " I was waiting for you Rubal and you have done a very big mistake by coming here, now I will kill you and take your stone, and by the way welcome you all to "Head Quarter of WhiteWash Venom" or you can say it a secret castle it is as big as your school.

You killed my Mom and Dad, you killed 7% of the world's superheroes and because of you, many superheroes were myrtle! just because you want to be immortal! Cried Rubal

No! Rubal, we can't let you die, said Abhishek, I will fight with him.

After that, greenish energy started forming around Abhishek but before Abhishek can attack WWV, WhiteWash Venom took out a stick on which there were 2 stones one was black and another one was red, WhiteWash Venom murmured something and a blackish colour circle came out and it hit to Professor Abhishek and he fell down

“Ahh...” Abhishek Murmured

Professor! Rubal and Mradu cried

Hahaha, you type of kids think that you will defeat me, but never this will be going to happen. WhiteWash Venom said

After that Abhishek again stand up, and at that time WhiteWash Venom said “Amon and Roman you both fight against these professors and I will fight against Rubal.

After that WhiteWash Venom moved his stick toward Rubal and a lot of red energy started coming out continuously towards Rubal, at that time a notification came on Rubal’s watch and there was written "activate the shield" and it appear on the right hand of Rubal, the next second the red energy touched Rubal shield and the red energy was too powerful that Rubal started dragging backwards and Rubal saw that cracks started coming on the shield and within few seconds the shield broken up and the red energy started hitting Rubal and he started feeling pain in this forefinger in which there was his ring

Ahhh... ouch... Rubal screamed

Then Rubal put his hand into his pocket and he found the pistol which his father gave him and then he move his hand in the direction where WhiteWash Venom was and he shoot an arrow towards Whitewash Venom and it hit his only shoulder and WhiteWash Venom stop attacking at Rubal and he took out the arrow from shoulder and flung him on the ground and said: “this small poison arrow can’t kill me!"

And again, Whitewash Venom took out his stick and was almost ready to attack again but suddenly Rubal started shouting very loudly “AHHHHHHHHHHHH” and his body colour started changing into purple and everyone at that time stops fighting and were watching Rubal, even WWS didn’t attack and was continuously staring Rubal. Soon, his hands, legs, face, hair, eyes and every other thing changes their colour to purple.

And after that a purple energy started coming out towards WhiteWash Venom from Rubal’s ring and then WWS also attack with his red energy, both energies were hitting each other

and soon WhiteWash Venom started dragging and purple energy started defeating red energy and at the same time Abhishek killed Amon and Mradu killed Roman and After that purple energy hits WWV and a big explosion happened there and it was too strong that the castle started shrinking and after that Rubal got fainted.

After 30 minutes

Rubal's eyes opened and he saw Monk, Blaze, Sherlin, all the professors and a lot of students standing near the bed where Rubble was lying.

Well done Rubal, I am proud of you, said Monk

Thanks, Rubal, you saved our lives today said Blaze and Sherlin at once

Di-Did, WWS died? Asked Rubal

NO, he was almost dead but he teleported to his world, said, Monk

Oh no! said Rubal

Don't worry Rubal, today you have done a very great thing and you are the first to defeat WWS said, Professor Abhishek

After this, there was a party organised by Monk for Rubal and he also got 10000 points for his bravery.

While Denial got disappeared somewhere and was not seen after that.

THE END...

GLOSSARY

(1) Murky - dark and gloomy

(2) Grinned - smile

(3) Scurry - move hurriedly

(4) Permit - allow

(5) content - Happy

(6) thrilling - excited

(7) Murmured - say something in a low or indistinct voice

(8) perplexing - mysterious

(9) screaming - Shouting long

(10) momentous - important

(11) sensation - feeling

(12) lament - crying

(13) quiver - shaking

(14) Wickedness - evil

(15) Flung - throw forcefully

(16) fragments - pieces

(17) misjudge - underestimate

(18) worthy - deserving

(19) Stared - look fixedly at someone

(20) regulate - control

(21) hush - silence

(22) demolish - destroy

(23) thrash - attack

(24) immorality - evil

(25) Robust - strong

(26) plummet - fall

(27) chuckle - laugh quietly or inwardly

(28) habitual - ordinary

(29) Raze- completely destroyed

(30) sorrowful - sorry
(31) arduous - difficult
(32) witless - stupid
(33) hollow - hole
(34) obligated - excited
(35) struck - hit
(36) tackling - attack
(37) visualize - imagine
(38) Combat - fight
(39) tremendous - very large
(40) gigantic - huge
(41) anxiety - worry
(42) blaring - loud
(43) valiantly - bravely
(44) Bravo - brilliant
(45)splendid - superb
(46) retrieval - rescue
(47) commandeer - hijack
(48) glimpsed - saw
(49) inadequate - bad
(50) Blare - loud
(51) regretful - sorry
(52) naive - innocent
(53) horrific - horrible
(54) Sumptuous - superb
(55) Giggling- laughing
(56) hostile - negative
(57) frightened - scared
(58) Remorse - guilty
(59)Demeanour - bad behaviour
(60)irate - angry
(61) whispered - murmured
(62) torn - teared

(63) dupe - fool

(64) shrieked - shouted

(65) Pester - disturbed

(66) stunned - shock

(67) miserable - sad

(68) yanks - pull

(69) Fled - run away

(70) divulged - revelled

(71) cloak - a sleeveless outdoor overgarment that hangs loosely from the shoulders.

(72)Sneer - Evil smile

(73)Paranoid - suspicion

(74) pursue - chase

(75) Peeved - irritate

(76) laborious - a lot of hard work

(77) Drowsy - tired

(78) Fatigue - exhausted

(80) furlough - rest

(81) astonished - surprised

(82) hastily - fast

(83) fritter - waste

(84) Shrieked - shouted

(85) Obliterate - destroyed absolutely

(86) Dawned - understood

(87) sedated - calm (someone) or make them sleep

Printed by Libri Plureos GmbH in Hamburg,
Germany